T0368692

I'm bleeding

Vitna Kim

WESTBOW
PRESS®
A DIVISION OF THOMAS NELSON
& ZONDERVAN

WestBow Press books may be ordered through
booksellers or by contacting:

WestBow Press
A Division of Thomas Nelson & Zondervan
1663 Liberty Drive
Bloomington, IN 47403
www.westbowpress.com
844-714-3454

Interior Image Credit: Sion Kim (cover artist)

ISBN: 979-8-3850-3890-9 (sc)
ISBN: 979-8-3850-3889-3 (e)

Print information available on the last page.

WestBow Press rev. date: 11/23/2024

PREFACE TO THE READER

Questions, questions, the questions you carry.

Do not doubt them, do not hide them.

Ask away, boldly.

Ask away, sincerely.

You may be surprised--of what comes your way.

What comes, your merry way.

My real home, where is it?
There it is, I have found it.

Contents

Part One: Immersed 1

Part Two: Swimming...51

Part Three: Lifeboat 129

"Mom, I'm bleeding."

Her mother takes one look at her, then leaves the room.

Part One: Immersed

1

Eva was six when she first felt her heart break.

She remembers it being subtle, but deep.

Her father would be in the little corner of their living room, drinking.

What exactly, she doesn't remember. But she just remembers that he would bring a cup of glass to his mouth and then gulp a few times, then pass out.

Sometimes he would sing himself to sleep, slurring lyrics to a long lost someone.

She would go up to his laid out body and kneel next to his ear. With her small hands, she would touch his sweaty head. Sometimes he would flinch, but most times, he would stay still.

"Dad, are you okay?"

"Appa, wake up."

He wouldn't answer. Sometimes he would startle himself, then crawl back into his knees, holding them tight.

Watching her father crawl into a ball, would do something to her heart.

Her father, her hero.

So small, so defeated.

2

Eva grew to understand that her father, her hero, sometimes was not there for her. He would be present physically, his head, his torso, his arms and legs–but he himself, would not be there. He would be gone. Gone to where exactly, she didn't know. But he would be gone.

He would show up sometimes, out of the blue. Whether it was a crisp hundred dollar bill handed, a togo order, or a car uptune–he would show up.

Then he would be gone again.

Eva grew to know her father as one shell of a person. He had all the attributes of a real person, a human, and yet nothing seemed to be graspable. She could not grasp, get a hold of, her own father.

She came to understand and later accept that people were not meant to grasp, or get to know.

She learned that the name father was just a title. Something we attach to a man who impregnates his seed into a woman. Just the seed of his being, warrants the requirement to call him father.

Alright, so she decides.

I have a father. I don't know him. I don't know him at all.
But he is my father.

My father.

Eva grew to meet many people. People of different ages, ethnicities, heights, and so on. One thing she could not shake was her dire need to keep people at bay. One step, two steps, okay pause. A third step, okay wait. No more. It was nice to meet you, farewell.

Two feet distance, was where she spent most of her years. Sometimes three, sometimes four. Very rarely, one.

She came to know her world as one where people were always two feet away, or further. Sometimes not even in the same room, the same house.

Knowing this as her world, it was odd when people began to inch closer. She didn't get it. What was the point of it. Of inching closer than two feet?

She was fine, living two feet away from people.

Wasn't she?

4

Eva met a guy one day.

She was drawn to him from the start. Something about the way he was, made her feel at home. The way he would be elusive, difficult to pinpoint. To grasp. It drew her in.

He would be here one moment, and gone the next.

This familiarity, it eased her, somehow.

She gave herself to him, wholeheartedly.

As if, he would give her, what she wanted this whole time.

As if, he could give her, what she had been looking for this whole time.

A hold–finally, –a hold.

5

He was a handsome and tall guy. Muscular, and had gentle eyes. Had a sweetness to him that could be smelt from a mile away.

His mother had passed, and he had 4 younger siblings.

His father had seemed to be shortly away, for work or for someone else.

He was left to care for, the remains of a fracture.

His pain, might have drawn her in.

The dripping, red drops of it.

6

She gave herself to him.
Again and again.

Till she was sore and no more.

"What's wrong with you?"
He would ask.

"Why are you acting like that?"
He would say.

Each time, she wasn't sure of what to say.

Her mind would wander to a place where there was
no riddle.

No mangled riddle to solve, no unknown answer to brute out.

No confusion, no perplexity.

A place where she knew everything.

As her soreness grew unbearable, she came to realize something.

Her white cotton shirt, had become soaked.

Through the fibers, her heart had leaked out.

Keenly observing and absorbing his pain, his wants, and his pleases—she had taken her eyes, off momentarily of her own wound that was growing deeper everyday.

Now agaping, she could hardly breathe.
The coldness of her shirt had frozen her torso, and in turn her heart with it.

Perhaps she hadn't noticed until now, because of the piercing cold.

Her numbed heart and torso.

It was now as good as ice.

8

She woke up one day, feeling a bit different. Not like her usual self.

She goes to the bathroom and clicks up the lights.

It is so bright.

She sees a figure in the mirror.

It is her, but not her.

She goes a little closer, and leans in.

Her face is paler than usual and she is half her weight.

She stares at the two pupils staring back at her.

They are darker than the last time she had remembered them to be.

Beadier, than she last remembered.

Eva must have gone somewhere. Gone off, to a place far away.

Maybe she has left for good, or maybe she was still alive but just buried.

Buried in a warmer place.

A place where her feelings were not met with a long stare, a tilting of the head.

They were attuned to, heard.

Valued, and not condemned.

A toasty fireplace—it must be.

She clicks the lights off, and leaves her bathroom.

9

Her mother comes home one day, very angry.

From the front doorstep porch, Eva's peach fuzz catches the faint smell of her mother's fumes.

Her mother walks up the steps to her.

"Eva, your father and I are going to divorce. Which one do you want to go with?"

"Mom, what do you mean?"

"You know exactly what I mean, Eva. So which one? Hurry up, tell me."

"Mom, go where."

"To live with!"

Eva inhales deep and closes her eyes shut.

Irritated by the hesitancy of her daughter's answer, her mother grits,

"Come on Eva! Hurry up and tell me. What's taking so long? What are you ever going to do with that useless brain of yours? You act just like your father."

Her mother brushes past her, and slams the front door hard.

As her mother storms inside, Eva stares at their etched metal house number.

23, attached so securely on their wooden blue door.

And she wonders for the first time.

What might make a home.

10

The next night, her brother, who is only a few years older than her, gets off of work.

He comes home later than usual, his second shift must've dragged out longer than usual.

He walks in through the front door to find his father passed out in the corner of their living room. He takes off his work shoes, and heads to his father.

The corner of the living room reeks of alcohol.

Instead of beer, today there are green soju glasses. Four empty, and one almost.

A small clear shot glass is in his father's hand, carefully gripped.

He bends down to take the shot glass out of his father's hand, and his father jolts his eyes open.

"Son, leave it."

"Dad, you just passed out."

"Son, you know I love you, right?"

Her brother closes his eyes and faces the ceiling above, exhaling out through his nose.

His fingers now purple and white, he grips his father's shot glass tight.

"Dad, go sleep on your bed."

It falls on deaf ears. His father is already drooling—into a new land.

His son lifts him off the lonely wet floor, and back to his bed.

An unknown number calls Eva's phone early in the morning.

"Hello?"

"Hey! This is Abby. Long time no talk. Do you remember me?"

Frowning, Eva tries to remember.

"Abby, your brother's girlfriend? Well, now his ex."

"Oh, hey Abby. My bad, what's up?"

There's an uncomfortable pause.

"Your brother cheated on me."

Eva can feel her hard breathing through the phone.

"Oh. Uh my bad, Abby. I'm sorry that happened."

She pauses.

"How can he do that to me? To me!"

Eva pulls the phone off her ear.

"After everything I've done for him. How can he do that to me?"

Eva takes a deep breath and puts the phone back on her ear.

"I don't know Abby. I really don't know."

Abby's tone shifts.

"What do you mean you don't know? You're his sister aren't you? Why did he do it, why did he cheat!"

For a second, Eva's mind leaves her.

"Hello Eva? Tell me, tell me why did he cheat!"

For a split second, Eva has a hard time collecting her mind back.

"Uh, hey Abby. I'm really sorry."

Abby hangs up.

Eva drops her phone to her side, and inhales deep.

She looks up at the sky.

The sun is so bright today.

12

Eva gets home that day to an oddly quiet home.

There is no shouting, no name calling, and no new dents in the wall.

The house is oddly still.

Her mother's bedroom door is open, and she sees the back of her mother's gray head resting on her pillow. She must be sleeping.

Eva walks up to the door frame, then peers in closer.

She notices that her mother's once light green pillow, is now a deep dark green. Parts of her hair are wet, stuck to her forehead.

Soggy tissues are sprinkled around her bed.

She turns her head, and Eva catches a glimpse of her swollen pink eyes.

They're more swollen than usual today.

Eva turns the doorknob softly, closing her door.

13

The next morning, Eva wakes up to her mother humming in the kitchen. The smell of marinated beef flows through the house into her bedroom.

Her mother peeps her head in through Eva's door frame.

"Good morning, sweetie. I made braised beef stew for you. Come to the kitchen and eat breakfast."

Eva notices that her mother is not looking directly at her, but instead looking down.

She can still see the raised eyelids, pink.

Eva looks up to the ceiling and says,

"Mom I'm not that hungry today, thank you though."

Her mother leaves without saying anything.

The back of her figure seems smaller today.

Frailer, then Eva remembers.

14

Eva wakes up to the sound of her quiet walls whimpering.

Without having to open her eyes, she knows that it is her mother.

She turns towards the wall and presses her hand against the cool midnight wall.

The whimpering stops.
Then begins again.

Maybe her mother, for a moment, sensed that another soul was awake in the house, listening to her pain.

Eva wants to comfort her, but this is not the first time that she could not console her mother's pain.
Not wanting to disappoint her mother or herself again, she just pats the whimpering wall back and forth–ever so gently.

And soon falls asleep, into the dark night.

15

The birds chirp their early morning voices away.

The bright sun shines into Eva's room, through one slit of her breezy white curtains.

It is calm and bright.

She covers her face with her warm white covers, toasted by the ray's greeting.

Her eyelids are stuck together. She winces, from the hardened crust.
They feel expanded, sore, and raw.

She lets out a deep sigh, and turns over on her pillow. Her cheeks are met with wet fabric.

She pries her eyelids open, and stares out through her blurry vision.

A spider is in the corner of her ceiling, webbing furiously.

She wonders for a moment.

If it ever feels heavy too.

If it ever feels, the weight of this world on its tiny shoulders.

On its small body.

16

Her mother comes into her room, very gleefully.

"Eva, wake up honey. We're going to take a family picture all together. Put on your best dress, I can help you with your makeup and hair. We are thinking of going with a light blue theme."

Eva covers her swollen eyes with her arm.

"Mom. Isn't it too early?"

"When your mother tells you to do something, you do it Eva. Don't be so slow like your dad again. Come on, we will be waiting for you in the living room."

She then prances away from the door.

Eva lets out a deep sigh, and musters up enough force to pull herself out of bed.

She heads to her bathroom, clicking the lights on.

Her face is more swollen than she expected them to be, they are pulsing from the swelling.

She places both hands to her cheeks, trying to push in the swollenness.

But it doesn't work.

Keeping her hands on her face, she doesn't want to take those pictures today.

She doesn't want to sit next to her mother or father.

Or her brother and smile wide.

She'd rather, let her throbbing eyelids rest for the day.

17

Her mother, father, and older brother are sitting shoulder to shoulder outside.

On their worn-out brown leather couch, they are waiting for Eva. Matching in their light blue attire.

From left to right, it is her father, mother, then her older brother.

She is not ready yet, for she had just come out in her pajamas.

Her mother with her enlarged eyes tells her,

"Eva, go get dressed right now. We're all waiting for you."

Eva looks at her mother, with her swollen pale red eyes.

She notices that her mother's lips are a bright red today.

"Eva, here let me put some makeup on you, and help you get yourself together. Let's go back to your room."

Her mother gets up from her seat and walks towards her, grabbing her arm back to her room.

While being pulled, Eva stares at her mother.

Underneath her makeup—her eyes too—are swollen.

Her mother begins clipping Eva's hair back, exposing her tender face.

Eva stays still, hoping that she sees.

Hoping that she sees her swollen eyes.

Her mother hurriedly puts makeup on her face.

She doesn't see.

Eva realizes today, that her mother can't see.

18

It is Sunday morning, sunny and fluffy white clouds hang in the air.

Her mother frantically gets herself and her family ready.

Eva's face is not swollen today, only tender.

They are late for church.

They arrive at church, and the lot is packed.

Her father finds an empty spot, and pulls in.

Her mother cheers in her new dress,

"Okay, we're here. Thirty minutes late, but we're here!"

One by one, they each get out of their white SUV.

Her mother grabs her husband's hand.

She then tells Eva and her brother to hold each other's hands, walking in one horizontal line.

They approach the tall doors of the front entrance. People's pearly whites greet her.

Very friendly waves, handshakes, back pats, and elbow jabs.

Laughing, praising the Lord.

Eva lets go of her brother's hand and her mother's. She holds her own hands, behind her back.

The sermon today is odd.

The person in the pulpit is screaming.

Calling us sinners that deserve hell.

Her mother begins to bawl next to her.

Eva blocks out the screams and closes her eyes.

Her mind wanders away again.

The pulpit's voice, the background piano—all soon grow quiet.

She goes to another place, not too far.

Where questions aren't so hard.

Where answers come easy, and do not flutter away the moment she tries to grasp.

She stays there, until the closing song comes on.

19

Out in the lobby, groups of people are huddled together. Some holding babies, some holding coffee.

Many mothers are huddled elbow to elbow, displaying their new bags. Some wear it high on their shoulders, some hold them out in their hands subtly.

Eva sees her mother, trying to start a conversation with one of the mother's standing.

Her worn out black bag from the thrift store hung over her shoulders.

The started conversation falls on silence, met with concerned eyes.

It must've been new for them.

For someone with a thrifted bag, to approach them.
An outer circle.

The demographic of the lobby looked really nice.
Almost inhuman.

There was an air of constriction—no room for a
misstep, no affordability for any mishaps.

Arrows of eyes were everywhere on her body.

Did she breathe wrong?

Eva swallows her dry throat.

Leaving out the large marble lobby room, an older lady smiles from the front entrance.

She smiles at Eva with large veneers.

The smile feels uncomfortable, forced.

The lady manages to get out through her teeth,

"God loves you."

Eva stares at her dull eyes, confused.

This lost room of grace.

Love?

Part Two: Swimming

20

The following week after that Sunday, Eva's home environment becomes worse.

Her mother cried more.

Her father drank more.

Her brother recycled more girls.

She wanted to leave this earth, more.

One thing was different though.

Now there was an open bible on their kitchen table. A brand new one, wide open.

As the days would pass, the thin pages would wilt and wither up.

Curled from the weight of her mother's tears.

The ink would spread into little blue puddles.

Useless, the pages seemed to Eva.

They seemed to be a table filler, just a prop—a silent deaf ear to real throbbing pain.

Eva was over it.

21

The family is gathered around their light wooden dining table today, on the menu is grilled meat.

The mother is cutting the juicy thick strips, the father pouring himself another glass.

Her older brother is on his phone.

Eva looks down at her plate and sees a small red outline of a heart, in ketchup.

Her mother places a sizzling grilled meat next to it. Careful not to smudge it.

"Aren't we a happy family?" She cheers.

Dead silence.

It is so awkward.

Her father is committing suicide every day, alone in the dark little corner of their living room.

Her mother is crying her stomach out every night, alone in the little corner of her room.

Her brother is catching and throwing women, back out to sea almost weekly.

The years of pent up, unspoken, and pushed down emotions must have had their full share.

Disregarded feelings of pure hatred.

Towards themselves, and one another.

Happy family?

Happy?

Family?

22

"Oh praise the Lord! I am so happy that our family is so happy. I wouldn't have it any other way."

Her mother seemed to be wanting to have it, another way however.

"There's nothing I wouldn't give, for our happy family."

She was losing her heart and mind everyday.

Her mother must've forgotten the bucket full of tears that she had shed almost daily, until the rising sun.

The ice spoons in the freezer, the sunglasses, the fluffs of tissue—everywhere.

The whispers of suicide.

The rotted and rotting walls, from the evaporation of her salt drops.

Her mother seemed vacant sitting across from Eva on that wooden table—gone.

Maybe her mind had evacuated, maybe it couldn't handle it.

This odd situation, Eva is not sure if she can continue.

Taking part, playing.

One thing Eva knows for sure is that they are dying.

This utter facade of feelings, actions, and words.

This made up reality that was not here.
Only in the minds, of those who believed it.

Of those who called wrong right and right wrong.

They are dying but they want to grill meat. Buy new clothes for Sunday. Plaster themselves with the words–happy and free.

They were not happy, or free.

This house made up of smoke.

Built on mere words, evaporating away by the minute.

Leaving all tenants unstable, leaving them to fall through sand.

The rising gas of carbon monoxide had reached its peak.

This house was burning.

23

Eva can't sleep that night.

The walls of her room feel six feet closer in than yesterday.

Enclosing each side of her white bed frame, the beige walls seem to her ears now.

She can't breathe.

She rests down on her pillow and scopes across her ceiling.

The spider is gone, same with its webs.

The carbon monoxide must've killed it, cinching its pure silked web along with it.

For a second in her quiet room, Eva wants to hang herself.

24

Through the darkness of her room, she sees mold on her beige walls.

It is seeping through.

This house had been rotting.

Burning–about to crumble.

What could she do?

What should she do?

Not knowing the answer to her own question Eva forces her eyes shut, coercing herself to sleep.

Allowing the burning walls to collapse on her limp body.

25

She wakes up in the middle of the night, unable to breathe again.

Rocking her fists, she hits her sternum.

One breath.

A second breath.

A third gasp.

Her eyes are burning from the smoke.

She grabs her chest and coughs.

She doesn't know what to do.

Stay and die.
Or leave and live.

Today, she is not so sure.

26

She decides to leave.

She packs a black school book bag and a small suitcase.

Going through her drawers, she gathers her underwear and socks.

Grabbing an outfit that is a little warmer than what she has on, she pulls it off the hanger and throws it into her bookbag.

She grabs her toothbrush and paste from her bathroom counter.

She throws them in on top of her clothes.

She packs her gray laptop, phone, and chargers for both.

Her social security card and high school diploma, she carefully slides it into the bag's back sleeve.

Maybe she will need them someday.

She stuffs her favorite pillow and blanket into her open suitcase.

She zips up both baggages.

As she zips up all the needed zippers, she blankly stares at her bed.

Still wet from the agony of last night.

Standing up, she takes one last long look at her room.

This room that had endured it all with her.

She kisses the cold glass of her surviving white betta fish and whispers.

"I have to go."

She observes its white flowing fins moving, oblivious for its soon coming death.

She puts her narrow feet in the navy blue slippers
her father had bought her recently and quietly exits her
home.

With two luggages tightly gripped in hand,

With zero clue, zero idea—of how she will live on.

27

Her car is very cold in the middle of night.

She turns it on, praying that it doesn't make a loud sound.

It does anyways, and she reverses out of her parking spot.

As she waits for the front gate to open, she looks back to the small rectangular window of her kitchen. The light is still on, she must've left it on after taking a water bottle from a cabinet.

The gate buzzes open, and she turns forward.

It is dark and quiet outside.

The neighborhood is fast asleep.

She is reminded of the metal etched 23 number on her wooden blue door.

How it was hanging on for dear life.

And now here she was, hanging onto hers.

28

At the first red light, she zones out.

She can't believe what just happened.

She grabbed two luggages and left.

The light turns green.

She can't believe she just left.

The lights turn back to red.

She can't believe she just left.

The empty streets and zero cars let her stay braked at the turning lights for a long time.

Maybe a few minutes.

29

She wakes up to a lit ray of moon shining her face, through the fogged wet windshield of her car.

Squinting and covering her eyes with her sleeve, she turns back over to sleep.

Now that she's already awake, her cold stiff limbs remind her of how difficult it was to fall asleep.

It's dark outside, and she forgets where she had last parked.

All she remembers is that she was last at a park. One of the ones she would go to as a child.

She must've driven here and passed out under a large tree.

She checks her dying phone and it's 3:20 am.

As she looks at the hanging moon, she exhales an icy dragon's breath through her two nostrils.

Warming her hands between her tired thighs, she dozes back to sleep.

30

Birds chirp through her windows.

She shields her face with both arms and her alarm rings.

It is already 6:00am.

She hits herself awake, and heads to class.

On the way to school, she notices how bright and clear the sky is today.

She turns left into her school parking lot, and finds a corner spot by the garbage bins.

The smell of her own body suddenly hits her nose.

She pulls her book bag out and tussles through, looking for her toothbrush and paste.

Clutching them with her hand, she heads to campus.

With her body close, she finds the restroom furthest away.

31

In class, her teacher is oddly joyful today.

It's early and he must've had a good morning.

He begins talking about education. The hard work and effort we must put in, if we want to succeed.

Eva falls asleep into her cozy arms.

The sound of notebooks closing and pens clicking off, wake her up.

Class is over, and she's the only one left.

The teacher's soft gray eyes meet hers and smiles. He nods his graying beard slightly.

She stands up, checking her pocket for her toothbrush and paste.

Holding it secure, she leaves the classroom.

32

A few weeks after staying in her car, she decides for the first time to ask for help.

If she continues to let her pride prevent her from asking for help, she sees herself being stuck in this situation for much longer than needed.

She asks one of her teachers if there are any dorms nearby, or resources that could help her.

Her teacher links her up with a nearby at-risk youth organization.

Intake interview goes, and she is accepted.

They give her guidance and emotional support for the week.

Breathing out, she can live on for another week.

33

The week of help comes to a quick end.

The inn room she had been placed in, was ending its hospitality soon.

In a few days, she will be out again.

She needs money.

For a moment, she thinks to sell her body.

Then another moment falls upon her.

She imagines an unborn child being taken from her womb.

Then another, and another.

Adding the pain of a child into this situation, brings her to close that thought tight.

She prepares to look for a job that doesn't risk the possibility of a pregnancy.

Mustering enough strength, she gets up on her faint legs.

And begins her day searching for a place that will hire.

Rejection after rejection hits her tired soul.

Maybe desperation could be smelt from a mile away. Maybe they saw something in her that she didn't yet.

Her slow but deteriorating will to live.

34

The very last day of her stay, she wakes up to itchy inflamed skin.

Bed bugs must've gotten to her.

She pulls herself out of the crowded bed.

Grabbing a packet of expired apple cinnamon oatmeal, she pulls out her ceramic mug from her bookbag.

Her ceramic mug has pastel outlines of butterflies with the thin words,

"Be The Change" engraved on it.

As she wipes the grooves with her dry thumbs, she stares off at the dull green walls of her room.

She rips open the oatmeal packet and empties it out into the mug.

Not having milk or bottled water, she turns on the old bathroom faucet. It sputters at first, then flows freely on the top dry layer of the oats.

At about halfway, she puts it into the rusting black microwave near the bathroom.

The oats rise, and soon the dim room begins to smell like spicy apples.

35

It is still dark out and the curtains of her inn are a thick and shiny copper gold.

There is another door right next to the front door that seems to connect to the next room over.

It has a big metal lock on it and is a lighter brown color than her door.

She hears a low hum of music coming from under.

Then a young girl's giggle.

Then a quiet moaning.

For a second, Eva loses her appetite.

Tying her hair up, she prepares for another day of job hunting.

36

She soon learns that posted signs of hiring does not necessarily mean that they are looking for a desperate new hire.

Rejections after rejection, greet Eva again.

By the middle of the day, Eva begins to grow discouraged.

The thought of opening her legs come up again.

She punches her steering wheel, and screams.

The thought of having no steady shelter, or money makes her mourn.

She is back in her car.

As she reverses out of the inn parking lot, she realizes something.

That things must always come to an end, sooner or later.

Then the pain—must too.

Very soon now,

Very soon.

The day is blazing and she decides to park the rest of her day under the same large tree– that she had fallen asleep under that one night.

As the day cools, the air turns cold very quickly.

She closes her windows, and wraps herself with the blanket that she had brought from home.

Her stomach burps, letting her know that it is hungry.

The calm park is very different at night.

After the families and children leave, other desperate souls begin to wander in.

Some naked, some only half clothed.

Most are nodding off, whether by themselves, a few others, or their dogs.

Someone's heavy hand knocks on her locked fogged up driver's seat window.

Pretending to be asleep under her blanket, she stays dead motionless.

The bored hand stops, and she soon dozes off into the night.

39

She wakes up to the noise of children cackling and laughing.

Metal swings, swinging up high.

Neon balls, bouncing on the pavement.

Squinting at the time, it is noon.

Her body has already thawed from the strong rays of the morning.

She sees two children in front of her windshield, running.

One is a few years older, and one is younger.

They are chasing each other with rosy chubby cheeks.

For the first time,

She thinks of her brother and misses him.

40

Smiling at the two running children, she zones out to the time of her own childhood.

The dirt holes dug in the front yard of their porch, some small, some massive.

The tomato plants, the sunflowers, the grasshoppers laying their eggs in due time.

The tattle-taling, staying up late watching their parent's new TV, and climbing from door frame to door frame.

For a second Eva forgets her burping stomach, thirsty throat, and time.

She falls asleep on her warm childhood bed.

41

One day she drives past a tattoo shop.

She decides to walk in and ask if they are looking for any help.

On the spot, she gets hired.

She begins working as the front desk receptionist.

Day in and day out, she checks in and out numbers of people.

A small inkling of hope arises from within her.

She can buy food now.

She can save some money now.

42

She holds the first paycheck of her job tight to her chest.

It is burning hot in her car, but she doesn't care.

She has earned enough funds for possible rent.

She places the white envelope carefully onto her warm passenger seat.

Reversing out of the parking lot, she doesn't know where to drive next to.

She doesn't mind today though.

She drives on forward.

43

She finds a small room up for rent.
Meeting the owner, she gets approved.

She brings her black bookbag, and suitcase into her
new room.

It is small, but she is so happy.
The carpet stinks, but she is so happy.

She unloads her small load of clothes out of her bag.

There is a little corner closet. It is the only floor
that has a red brick lay pattern. The past tenant had left
three white wire hangers hanging on the rail. She slips
her dirty clothes onto them.

Beaming, she hangs them on—one by one.
Bending to sit her worn ankles down, she gets a
whiff of old feet.

Squeezing her nose closed, she smiles.
She plops her entire body down, and rolls around.

Cheesing to herself hard, she wonders if this is what heaven feels like.

This must be heaven.

She is in heaven today.

44

It is a slow day at work today.

Only two people have come in so far, both guys.

One asks for a dragon on his back, while another asks for a little dinosaur on his left ankle.

Eva smiles at their friendship.

The dinosaur one winces, while the dragon one giggles the entire time.

Interesting, she thinks.

How differently one can cope with pain, from each other.

45

Another client walks in after the two friends leave.

She is wearing a tight black tank top, layered under a bright neon yellow one.

It is dirty, and there are holes.

She's wearing torn tight shorts, jean blue.

Her legs are tan from the sun, light pink sores filling up every inch of tired skin.

She has piercing blue eyes.

Her hair is knotted in a greasy bun.

She slurs something under her breath but Eva can't catch what she is saying.

"Hello, how can I help you today?"

Blinking and swaying, while weakly scratching her matted head, she seems drowsy today.

"Did you want a tattoo today?"

She has dried, brown tear streaks down her grimy cheeks.

Eva looks down at her belly and sees that she's pregnant.

Her feet are unwashed in pink sandals–swollen.

She rests her purple bruised hands on her protruding hip. She closes her eyes, and her head falls onto her shoulder.

She falls asleep standing up.

Eva gets up from her chair, and walks around the black marble counter to her.

She puts her hands on her sun-kissed bare shoulders, and leads her gently to the door.

Her swollen feet follow, the sandals hitting her dry soles.

Outside, she is still standing with her eyes closed.

"What's your name?"

She opens her eyes, the blue shining out.

With her head still dropped to her shoulder, she breathes out,

"Crystal."

"Where are you from, what are you doing here, Crystal?"

Before Eva can hear Crystal, her manager calls her in.

A new client needs to be checked out.

Before she heads back in, Eva pulls out a crumpled twenty from her pocket.

She places it in the middle of Crystal's bruised palm.

46

That same day, another someone walks in.

This time he is an older man, rough around the edges. He is wearing a stained orange hoodie, his baseball cap matching with it exactly.

He's angry.

His eyes are bulging, and his jaw is clenched.

"Hi, how can I help you today?"

He ignores Eva and walks past the marble counter, straight into the shop.

She sees that he is gripping something in his hand.

It is a brown beer bottle.

He walks up to someone getting a tattoo, and stares.

At the person getting it, and the tattooist.

They both pretend he's not there and ignore him.

He says something, but it's mumbled.

He puffs his shoulders up, and brings his fist up.

They both ignore him again.

He brings his fist down, and brings the other hand up–chugging down the last remaining liquid.

He's swaying and stumbling his way through the shop.

He then sees Eva staring at him from the front marble counter, smiling.

He walks towards her.

"Do you like tattoos?"

He unclenches his jaw, and slides the brown beer bottle into his hoodie pocket.

His bulging eyes soften.

Revealing one missing front tooth, he replies,

"Yes."

47

She goes home to a quiet place.

The landowner lives in the other half of the house, with her husband and three kids.

Today, they are really quiet.

Usually one of them is crying.

She takes her shoes off, and walks over to her locked room door.

Opening it, she drops her little leather backpack on the carpet next to her door frame.

She lets out all the accumulated sighs of her day.

Her room is bone bare.

Right below the broken window blinds, is her laid out blanket from home.

Her favorite pillow is taking up space in that same corner.

She kneels and rests her palms on the bumpy sour blanket.

She exhales and lays the rest of her body down.

Looking up at the ceiling, she sees two spiders. Furiously webbing.

This house doesn't seem to have carbon monoxide.

Nor does it seem to be rotting.

It seems a good place to grow.

Eva knocks out from her long day.

48

The next morning, she wakes up to kids screaming.

They're in the kitchen, fighting over who gets to eat the first cookie their dad made.

Eva gets ready for work.

At work, it's very busy.

Music is loud, people are coming in and out.

A young lady wearing a brown leather jacket comes in.

She has many face piercings.

Her nose, both eyebrows, and the middle of her lip.

She has soft green eyes.

"How can I help you today?"

She stares long at the blooming plant on the counter.

"I came in to get my tongue pierced."

Behind her a towering man and smaller woman walk in.

A little girl is holding onto the lady's leg.

"Sure, can I have your name?"

"Cassidy."

The man from behind comes up next to her.

Grabbing her chin between his thumb and four fingers, he pulls her face to his.

"Where on your tongue are you getting it pierced again?"

Cassidy flinches.

She shows him her white tongue, and points with her pale finger where she wants it pierced.

He grabs the collar of her leather jacket, and lifts her up to his height.

"Honey, stop." The lady from behind comes next to Cassidy and pulls her back down from the man's grip.

"I can do whatever I want to."

Cassidy is now blushing red, contrasting her light green eyes.

The eyes of the little girl on the mother's leg widen, her hazel eyes expressing themselves.

She frowns her light peach eyebrows while looking at the man next to her mother.

She then hides between her mother's pants.

49

Another client comes in towards noon.

She wants a 3D noose on her neck.

After that client, another one comes near three.

She wants her nipples removed.

Another one after that,

Wants his eyes tattooed.

The last final client of the day,

Wants to kill himself.

50

The landlord's husband is in the kitchen cooking dinner for his family. Sweet and frothy chicken soup.

Eva runs into him wearing his spotted purple apron after she gets home from work.

With both hands in heat mittens he smiles at Eva.

"Working hard?"

She sighs and nods at him.

She goes into her room.

Today her room feels hollow.

She misses her father.

The small thud of children's feet enter into the kitchen in a rhythm.

The three children fight over who gets to sit next to their dad.

She feels so lonely today.

The lit moon passes in through the cracked blinds. It is quiet and dark outside her window.

She wants to kill herself today.

Part Three: Lifeboat

51

It is way past twelve o'clock, and the house and kids are sleeping.

Eva is on her bumpy blanket, eyes blinking in the dark.

The pillow under her head begins to move.

She thinks it is her head pulsating at first, so she ignores it.

Then something starts to move under her pillow.

Half of her gets up and yanks the pillow up.

There is a gigantic dark brown cockroach, wobbling its long antennas back and forth.

She has never seen one that big–in her life.

So surprised, she can't even scream.

She stands up and turns the lights on.

Bending to pick up her favorite pillow, she leaves the house to her car outside.

It's very windy outside.

The night felines greet her with their glinting eyes.

She hops into her car, and stuffs the pillow behind her head.

Then dozes off under the brightly-lit moon.

52

That night must've been tiring, because she doesn't wake up on time for work.

Her phone is in the room with the cockroach.

Usually she would have been frantic that she had woken up late, but today she isn't.

For some reason, she feels a sense of calm today.

She doesn't care if she makes it to work or not.

She stretches her compressed spine out on her seat, and lets out a yawn.

She doesn't care anymore.

Maybe not caring was the answer.
The answer to no disappointment or crushed expectations.

For some reason today, she feels alive.

53

She shows up to work the following day that she is scheduled.

Her manager asks her where she was yesterday, and why there was no communication.

Eva ignores him.

A client asks where the bathroom is.

Eva ignores her.

Her father messages her out of the blue in seven months.

Eva ignores him.

A cop follows from behind, on her way home.

She ignores him too.

At home, the three kids say hi to her sitting around the dining table.

She ignores them.

54

In the quiet of her locked room, she is met with a certain wave.

A wave of guilt—an ocean of it.

How and when, did she turn so heartless? So cold?

She didn't feel anything to her manager's genuine question, the first-time client asking for where the bathroom was, when her father messaged her for the first time in seven months, when the police was following from behind.

Especially when the landlord's three children greeted her so innocently and cheerfully, she didn't feel anything.

The numbness must've lost its gauge, it was just numb now.

The guilt and shame of being so cold soon encapsulates her weary mind.

Alone in her room,
She really wants to kill herself today.

55

She opens her narrow closet, with the red brick floors.

She slides the few worn outfits over, and makes room on the chipping rail.

She pulls her blanket off the floor, and twists it between her palms. It twists, and turns.
She rolls it tight, into a thin piece of fabric.

Her vision is blurry, she cannot see through the water that is welling.
Drops of salt fall down her dry cheeks.

She blinks both eyes hard, the rest of the salt landing.

Her lips begin to quiver, but she bites them down hard to quiet them.

She wraps her skinny neck around three times, tying a knot on the fourth.

Her narrow bare feet touch the icy bricks of her closet floor.

She loops the fabric around the railing and ties a strong last knot.

Swallowing her spit one last time, she constricts herself.

She begins to gasp.

Blood rushes to her head, and her eyes cry.

She bites her tongue down.

Tasting the bitter blood of her own body.

Flailing now, her feet flutter.

Her mother's face appears.

Then her father's.

Then her brother's.

Eyes rolling back, she passes out.

56

She wakes up to her bottom freezing.

She had fallen down from the railing, and was now laid out on the hard brick floor of her narrow closet.

She doesn't remember what she just did.

Her neck is sore, and there is something constricting her windpipe.
She reaches up, and finds her soft blanket around her neck.

She doesn't have the energy to untie it, so she just leaves it alone.

Sitting up, she grits her teeth in pain from her spine getting out of its fallen position.

She hears the footsteps of one of the children running towards her door.

"Miss Eva? We have something for you! Are you home?"

Eva exhales deep, letting her eyes close themselves.

She helps herself up, grabbing the walls of her closet.

Turning the knot behind her neck, she turns the door knob open.

"Surprise!"

It is three of them, holding a small paper plate together.

In the middle was a carefully placed homemade cupcake.

Squiggled in blue, was the uppercase letter E.

"We made one for you Miss Eva, do you like it?"

Their small lips covered in cake batter, stretched as far wide as possible.

Six pupils large and expectant, waiting for her response.

Eva looks at their powdery shirts and lifts out her hand.

She takes the paper plate from their chubby fingers.

"Oh my, wow. Good job guys, I'm going to eat all of this yummy cupcake right now."

The older one grins big, and runs off to the living room. The other two follow suit.

Eva looks down at the squiggled blue E on the plate.

Her lips begin to quiver.
She closes the door with her elbow.

57

She doesn't want to eat the cupcake.

It is so precious.

Uneven and lumpy as it was, three hearts had just been poured out onto them.

How could she take even one bite out of it?

She holds the bottom of the plate with two open palms, for a good while.

Drips of gratitude, begin dropping.

Liquifying the blue E, now into a muddy E.

Looking up at her ceiling she closes her wet eyes.

Grateful to be alive.

58

Her father messages her.

It has been a while since she had last spoken with him, or looked him in his eyes.

His number pops up on her phone screen, and her face turns white forgetting to inhale.

Why on earth would her dad text her?

Out of blue?

She turns her phone over on the dark carpet and the lit screen illuminates it.

It stays lit for a few seconds, then goes dark.

In the pitch black room, legs crossed close to her chest—she rests her heavy head on the wall behind her.

Banging it in light thuds, she tries to make sense why her father has just messaged her.

There are now four spiders in the corner, webbing furiously.

They must've reproduced from the abundance of oxygen in the room.

In her pitch black room, she enters into her pitch black mind.

Eyes closed shut, she stays there for a good two minutes.

There is silence for another two.

Her phone buzzes again.

She turns it over, and her dad has messaged her again.

"Your car needs a smog check soon. Come home and drop it off this weekend."

Eva just stares at her screen.

Instead of joy, she feels a rage arise.

The times she had almost died, the times she had recreated the spitting image of her father through her men, the times she almost died. The boatloads of empty promises, of security.

She feels a certain heavy weight arise from within.

Of course under the rage, was a deep sadness.

A certain hurt, from her heart being let down again and again.

If what she had experienced from her father was love—she didn't want it.

The off and on, the random barging in and out.

Was she a dog? A pet, to keep on a leash? Give a few treats to lure back?

Alone in her room, Eva is very conflicted.

Why was she caring all of a sudden?

Hadn't she vowed earlier, not to?

She ignores her father's messages and gets ready for work.

59

At work, she can't seem to focus.

Her father's messages continue to float around in her mind, entering doors that she didn't even know existed there.

While greeting and booking in new clients, she feels a tinge of sadness.

Eva is sad.

She wants to speak to her father, but doesn't know how.

This slab of resentment she carries with her, she is not sure how to chip it. How to get rid of it.

It appears to have hardened without her knowing over the years, and now it is stone.

Stuck in her chest, hard.

She blasts the shop's music up.

Plunging herself into a much less complicated world.

The uncomplicated world of rhythm and flow.

Where every beat and tone– is labeled, known, and predictable.

60

She meets another guy at work.

He is a coworker and very charming.

The charm sweeps her off of her light feet.

His father had passed away a year ago, and he was the oldest out of two.

He reminds her exactly, of the past person she had given her whole heart to.

With no more pulse left in her heart for her to feel, she sleeps with him.

She wakes up to another man next to her in bed. She swears it was her coworker, but this morning he is a completely different person. He looks like a whole stranger she has never met before.

His charm must've gotten tired and worn out throughout the night.

61

She decides to drop her car off Saturday, to let her father smog check it.

She doesn't plan to stay or say hi. Only to drop off and come back in a few days to pick it up.

She pulls up to her old parking lot with ease. No one will be home as it is a Saturday—when work is most busy for her family.

After she parks her car, she steps outside.

Walking past the gate and a few miles down from her old house, a loud honk hits her from behind.

Startled, she scrunches her eyebrows and jerks her neck backwards towards the horn.

It is her white honda.

In the driver's seat, is a familiar face.

A way too familiar one.

The eyes staring back at her are determined.

Sharp, and directed.

It is her father.

He glides the four wheeler next to the pavement she is walking on.

He rolls the passenger seat's window down.

"Get in."

Eva doesn't know how to feel.

Anger?

Happiness?

Resentment?

She is beyond perplexed at this point.

"Get in."

Eva ignores him, and stares down at her worn out shoelaces.

She keeps walking.

He follows her.

Embarrassed, she ignores him and walks the opposite direction.

The sky is an odd bright blue today.

He U-turns and comes back to her.

"Eva, get in."

He looks frail. Half of his weight must've left him.

"Go back to work dad," she tells him through the traffic wind.

"Eva get in."

He is relentless today.

Relentless as his drinking routine.

Her tired hot feet persuade her to just get in.

Eva decides she will let him take her in the direction she was headed anyways.

It is so awkward in the car.

He rubs the steering wheel with both his calloused hands.

He grips, then smooths, then grips again unable to stay still.

"This car needs a cleaning, Eva."

Eva can't believe her ears right now. Or what is even happening right now.

She stares out her window, wind in her face— counting how many people are out walking on the hot pavement.

"So, how have you been Eva?"

Eva feels something knocking, on the rock in her chest.

She usually feels nothing in there, but today there is a light tapping in her chest.

She can feel something sprout.

A little noiseless bud of hope–if you will.

62

He drops her off a few miles away from the rented room she is living in.

As she gets out, he hands her something.

It is the first time she has touched her father's hands that close.

The cracked and dry fingers brush her soft palm.

It is a crisp hundred dollar bill.

She gives it back to him.

"I don't need it."

His eyes sulk for a millisecond.

She shuts the door and walks away to her rented home.

63

Her father calls her a few days later.

"Hey Eva, it's dad. Your car is ready, everything passed. You can come pick it up, when you can."

She doesn't say anything and hangs up.

After the call, she stares off into space.

She blinks a few times, then another few times.

She wonders where her dad was, where he could've possibly been.

When her car broke down many times she racked herself into debt, when guys would catch and throw her heart back to sea, when her own hands would noose her?

Where was he?

Drinking? Singing?

Seducing and sedating himself at the same time, in that corner of the living room?

Putting on a sweet show, for all of them to watch?

She realizes this moment that resentment—runs rather deep in her now dense heart.

64

A familiar image smears over the grooves of her mind.

It is her father curled-up on the dusty floor of their old house.

Hugging his knees tight to his chest—rocking almost.

He is sniffling himself to sleep, to the tempo of an old lullaby.

Maybe his mother would sing that to him, or maybe his father.

Maybe his older sister.

But today he was singing to his own ears, to his own rocking body.

Maybe he—too—was longing for his father.

Maybe he—too—was longing for somebody.

65

The image of her father rocking himself to sleep disappears.

Eva decides to dial her father's number.

He picks up on the second ring.

"Hey dad."

He is quiet on the other end.

"Dad?"

After some hesitation he slurs in drunk saliva,

"Yes…Eva?"

Taking a deep breath, the deepest breath she has ever breathed, Eva opens her mouth.

"I love you dad."

He is dead quiet on the other end.

Then a quiet heaving.

Then a gulping sniffling.

Her father was crying.

"Love... me?"

66

Eva blinks both of her eyes, releasing two heavy drops onto her toes at the same time.

As the weight of those two drops leave her eyes, she feels somehow lighter.

Those two feeble drops seemed to take along with it, something that had never belonged to her in the first place—to begin with.

"Yes dad you. I love you."

He hiccups, burping out the alcohol in between his teardrops.

A wall of barricaded tears—of a long found grief—breaks open on the other end of the call.

Her father is now weeping into his phone.

Whether he was crying for her, or for a long lost somebody, she didn't know.

But it was the first time she had heard her father cry like that.

Like a young boy–grieving for his gone mother.

Eva gapes her eyes open towards her ceiling, trying to keep the pool of salt within her eyelids.

Placing her hand on her chest, she hangs up the call.

67

Alone in her room,

Eva wants to run to her father.

She wants to sprint.

Though miles down and away, she is willing to run her soles sore.

Barefoot or with shoes—it does not matter to her today.
She will run naked if she has to.

For the first time, she wants to give him a hug.

In his lonely corner of the living room.

In his suffering.

In his aching soul.

Today, she wants to soothe his aching and not condemn it.

68

For the first time, Eva realizes something.

Eva comes to understand—that people are meant to be known.

People are meant to be understood.

Known.

She learns that we are meant to be understood and known.

69

Eighteen years.

More for her father.
More for her mother.

More for her brother.

Of a longing.

Of a certain longing.

.

Of an absolute longing.

70

Eva realizes that she and her father both–have been starved of the same thing this whole time.

In desperate dire need of the same one thing.

And that was love.

1

2

3

Gratitude to the one who knew me from the beginning, and loved me.

Thank you Jesus

Author's Note

The idea for this book came to me, in the midst of great pain. Not knowing how to get this story out, I struggled quite a bit. I would begin, and then scrap it entirely.

Until one day, the story was screaming to be let out. So I gave it its wish.

While writing this book, I did not expect to get as emotional as I did. But now I have come to understand that revisiting old memories can be joyful on one hand, and very painful on the other.

For life itself, I am very grateful. Though I did not ask to be here, and though the journey has been quite a ride—I would not trade it for anything.

I'm not sure if I would repeat it, or if I would have any remaining strength left to survive this again—but regardless I am very grateful for the lessons I have learned.

Thank you pain, thank you understanding—you have brought me to a new revelation of myself and this world we live in.

About the Author

Vitna Kim lives in Orange County with her family. She enjoys nature, and speaking of mending broken hearts and relationships through the one who is love. "I'm bleeding" is her first written book.

Printed in the United States
by Baker & Taylor Publisher Services